Turkey Grove

Steve Lemasters

A NOTE TO READERS

This novella is the first of a series intended to describe the most beautiful area of Florida, the land on the south shore of Orange Lake, now known as Citra.

Information about the land, Orange Lake and the orange groves came from first hand experience. The author grew up in Citra, Florida and worked in orange groves during summer vacations. He explored the dense woods on the south shore of Orange Lake and marveled at the burial ground mentioned in the book. He walked every inch of the Turkey Grove and felt the presence of the Indian who planted the trees.

Information about the Timucuan Indians came from Internet searches, including:

Timucuan.org
Fcit.usf.edu/florida/lessons/timucua/timucua.htm
En.wilkipedia.org/wilki/timucua

Good information on names for Timucuans was not available. Names commonly given for other Indians were used – something seen soon after birth.

If you enjoyed this novella, you will also enjoy the second book of this series, a novel titled, "Crosby's Turkey Grove."

Steve Lemasters

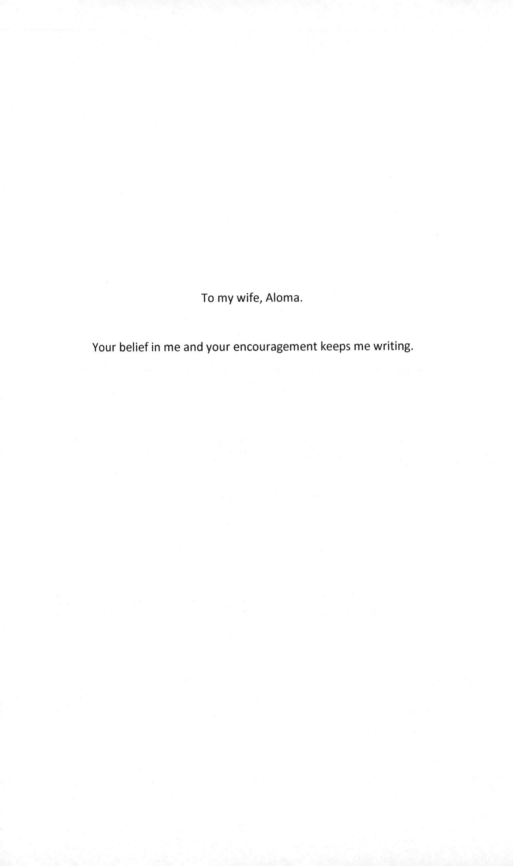

To my wife, Aloma.

Your belief in me and your encouragement keeps me writing.

CONTENTS

CONTENTS - CONTINUED

CHAPTER 1

Listening to the sounds coming from the hut, Running Bear sat with his head bowed. He asked the Great Spirit to protect Morning Flower and to give him a healthy son. He was worried.

Morning Flower had delivered their other two children quickly and without complication. Their first son, now six years old and a strong athletic boy, was already a leader among the children of the tribe. Their daughter, three years old, showed signs of being a beautiful and talented girl like her mother.

An old woman came from the hut and walked slowly to Running Bear.

"The baby is turned the wrong way. Morning Flower is having great difficulty. She is strong and trying hard, but we are afraid for her and the baby."

She reached out her hand and touched his shoulder and then slowly walked back to the hut.

A muffled scream came from the hut. Running Bear asked the Great Spirit for his help. Members of the Council came and sat with him. Each man assured Running Bear that everything would be all right and then left. He did not believe everything would be all right.

Finally, the old woman came out of the hut again.

"The baby has arrived. Come."

The look on the old woman's face told him that something was wrong. He entered the hut more frightened than he had ever been.

The crying baby was wrapped in deerskin. Morning Flower's hair was drenched with sweat. She was pale and could barely speak. She looked up and tried to smile.

"We have another son."

Then she closed her eyes.

The old woman whispered, "Morning Flower is bleeding. She may live. She may die. The boy came out feet first. One leg is broken and his hip is not in the socket. He will live, but he will not be able to run, or maybe even walk."

She touched the chief on his shoulder and said quietly, "I am sorry. I did all I could."

"Does Morning Flower know our son is crippled?"

"No, she is weak. Do not tell her today. We will know by morning if she will live. If she wants to see the baby tonight, we will keep the baby wrapped in deerskin so she can't see his legs."

Running Bear felt an emptiness he had never known.

He told the old woman, "The custom of the Timucuans is to kill a baby who is not normal. The clan cannot afford to feed children who will not grow up to be productive. I will wait until tomorrow to talk to Morning Flower about the baby."

He sat with Morning Flower all night. At daybreak she opened her eyes, looked around and smiled at him. Running Bear leaned over and kissed her cheek. She smiled again.

"I want to hold our baby boy."

Running Bear woke the old woman. She checked the baby and put it in the arms of Morning Flower. She kissed the baby and put him to her breast to nurse. "We must give our son a strong name," she whispered and then fell asleep.

After a while the old woman took the baby back to its pad. "Morning Flower will live. She won't recover for several weeks and will need help. It will be difficult for her when you tell her the baby is deformed and must be put to death."

Later in the afternoon Morning Flower woke and asked to see her husband. Running Bear was called. When he entered the hut, Morning Flower was nursing the baby, still wrapped in deerskin. She smiled at her husband and motioned for him to sit beside her.

"I know something is wrong with our son, but no one will tell me what it is. They keep him wrapped. What is wrong?"

Running Bear sighed. He took her hand.

"The baby didn't turn and came feet first. That's why your delivery was so hard. One of the baby's legs is broken and one hip is not in the socket. Our son is crippled."

Morning Flower put her hand over her mouth and gasped.

"Oh no. We must fix his leg and hip. We will fix him and he will be fine."

"Our custom is to send the soul of a deformed baby back to the spirit world to be born again. Our village cannot afford sons who are unable to hunt and fight."

Morning Flower unwrapped the deerskin from her son. A frown spread over her face as she examined the mangled leg. Running Bear watched with dread as a deep feeling of love overwhelmed Morning Flower and radiance replaced her frown.

"We will splint the leg so the bone heals, and we will bind the legs together to let the hip return to its socket. Our son will be fine."

"Our custom is to not take a chance. We must send him back to the spirit world," said Running Bear in a stern voice.

She held her son tightly.

"You will not kill my baby. I can feel something special about him. He will walk and someday he will be the most important person in our village. I will personally take care of him until he recovers. If there is not enough food, he can have my portion. If you kill him, I will kill myself."

Running Bear was not surprised. He knew his wife would never forgive him if he killed the baby. Yet, he had a responsibility.

"I will talk with the Council in the morning. They will help me decide what to do."

He left the hut.

Before the Council met, Running Bear talked with his wife again. She showed him the splint on the leg and how she had bound both legs together to straighten the hip.

"See how the leg is straight with the splint. The bones will grow together and be strong. The hip is back in the socket. Binding his legs together will keep the hip in its socket until it is healed. Within two moons, our son will be healed. He will grow up to be a strong boy like our other son."

"It is possible. I will talk with the Council," Running Bear agreed.

Running Bear, Fast Rabbit, Wise Owl and Singing Bird sat on mats in the community hut for their daily Council Meeting. Wise Owl was nervous as the others tasted the white drink for the purification ceremony. Normally Morning Flower prepared the traditional drink. Wise Owl's wife had the responsibility this morning. Before sunrise she selected the holly berries, crushed them and mixed the drink just as Morning Flower had taught her. Running Bear tasted the drink and nodded his approval to Wise Owl.

As he felt energy from the caffeine flow through his body, Running Bear spoke to the Council about his son.

"You have heard my son was born feet first. His leg was broken and one hip is not in the socket. I was prepared to send his soul back to the Great Spirit, but Morning Flower showed me she had mended the broken leg with a splint and put the hip back in its socket. She bound both legs together to keep the hip in place. She thinks our son will be strong and healthy. I'm not so sure. I don't know what to do."

Fast Rabbit frowned.

"Of course, she would say that. New mothers have an instinct to protect their babies. I have never seen a child with a broken leg recover completely. I recommend sending its soul to the spirit world as soon as possible."

Running Bear nodded and looked at Wise Owl.

"I want to hear your opinion," he urged.

Wise Owl took a long draw on his pipe before speaking.

"Fast Rabbit is correct. Our custom is to take care of this type of problem quickly. And it is the husband's decision, not his wife's decision. However, this situation is different. The boy is the son of our Chief. When there is a problem giving birth, sometimes the mother cannot bear more sons. The Chief has only one son. Do we want to take the life of a boy who might heal and someday grow up to be important to our village? I think our Chief should think about this carefully."

All eyes turned to Singing Bird.

"Morning Flower is a strong woman. I would not want to be the one to tell her we are taking the life of her new son."

Running Bear looked around the hut.

"Thank you for your help. I will tell you my decision tomorrow at our Council Meeting."

After the meeting Running Bear left the village alone and spent the day walking among the giant live oak trees in the dense hammock forest. Today, he was unaware of the moss swaying in the light breeze and hanging like a beard from the giant oaks.

Deep in thought, the Chief did not hear the singing of the birds or the chirping of the squirrels in the trees. He did not notice the sweet scent of the wildflowers where the sun penetrated the dense canopy of trees. Running Bear thought only about his son, his wife and his responsibility. He knew his decision would have serious consequences.

That evening Running Bear entered his hut and sat beside his wife. She smiled and held up their son.

"He's getting used to the splint. He seems to know this will help him. He's a real fighter."

"We discussed our son's problem in the Council Meeting this morning. There was no clear agreement. I have thought about what to do and have asked the Great Spirit for help. My decision is final."

Morning Flower felt a sense of dread. She started to speak but stopped when her husband raised his hand.

"I have decided to let our son live. I trust your judgment that he will heal and be normal. If he does not heal, he will be a future burden to our clan. He will eat without contributing by hunting or fishing. Other warriors will defend him because he cannot fight. He will never have a wife to care for him, so we will take care of him for the rest of our lives. When we are gone, the burden of his care will pass to our son and our daughter. Meanwhile, the talk of the village will say that I used my power as Chief to bend to your wishes rather than follow our tradition. I may lose respect in the village."

Morning Flower sat in grim silence and then spoke quietly.

"My dear husband, thank you for your decision. I will do everything to make sure our son heals. When he is a strong young man, people will look at your decision as wise and they will respect you for it. Our son will grow to be a leader of his people like his father. His name is Fighting Wolf because he is such a fighter and will have to fight hard to be strong. Do you approve of this name?"

Running Bear nodded and left the hut. He had a feeling he would regret this day.

CHAPTER 2

Morning Flower encouraged Fighting Wolf to take one more step. He struggled through the pain as he extended his bad leg and then put weight on it. His mother caught him and praised him.

"Good boy. You did it. You're getting better and better."

Fighting Wolf fought back tears.

"I don't want to do this. It hurts. My friends don't have to do it. Why should I?"

"Because you're special. You were born with a weak leg, and you have to strengthen it. Don't you want to run with the other children and grow up to be a strong warrior?"

"I do, Mommy. But it hurts when I take steps."

"We're done for the day."

She carried her son over to a play area and put him on the ground. As she returned to her hut tears formed in her eyes. She had been wrong to think Fighting Wolf would completely recover. He would always be a cripple. It broke her heart. Yet, he did have a fighting spirit. And he was brighter than her other two children at this age. He had a positive attitude and would do anything she asked. He was a perfect three-year old, except he was lame.

Her husband tended to ignore Fighting Wolf. At his birth, Running Bear listened to her plea and promise and allowed their son to live. When their son's leg didn't heal properly, the Council criticized him. He believed the people of the village had lost respect for him. He was depressed.

While they still slept under the same deerskin robe at times, no new sons or daughters came. Their relationship was cool. Her heart ached for Fighting Wolf, her husband and their relationship. She knew her life would never be the same.

CHAPTER 3

Fighting Wolf hobbled over to the other children of the village and grabbed his crutch that one of them had taken. He gave the thief a whack with his crutch and laughed.

"Don't forget, when I have my crutch, I can hold my own with any of you."

A few moons ago his father had shaped a tree limb so that he could put it under his arm when he walked. The crutch changed his life. Not only could he walk, he could run. He was not as fast as other eight-year old children could run but was fast enough to keep up.

Morning Flower came up to the group of children.

"Enough of that. No hitting with the crutch. Fighting Wolf come with me. We are going to the fields to inspect our crops."

He was enjoying playing but knew he must go with his mother. She had explained to him that because of his leg, he would not be a great warrior. Therefore he must contribute to the village in other ways. He needed to learn everything about the village. Fighting Wolf should be an expert in growing crops, hunting, fishing, building huts, laying out a village, understanding council meetings, healing, making weapons and making canoes. He must work hard to learn things about the village, to contribute to the village and to make his father proud of him.

As they were walking to the field, his mother asked, "Why do you think the crop of beans is especially good this year?"

Fighting Wolf paused for a moment.

"Everything seems to grow in the rich hammock land. The rain has been good this spring. Of course, we saved the best beans from last year's crop for seed. And we've kept the raccoons and birds out of the fields most of the time."

"Good answer, but how about when we planted them?"

"I forgot. We planted them on the second full moon after the shortest day of the year. And we were lucky, we didn't get any frost."

"Would we plant beans in the same field every year?"

Fighting Wolf thought for a moment.

"No, the old people in the village say if you plant the same crop in a field year after year, the beans will not grow well. It's best to plant beans one year and the next year plant corn."

"Very good. You're learning. Now let's pull some weeds out of the field. You forgot to mention that."

On their way back to the village after working in the field, Morning Flower had an assignment for her son.

"I want you to do three things before we work in the cornfield tomorrow afternoon. I want you to look at the outside of all the huts in the village and tell me which one is built the best. I want you to spend an hour with the flint shaper when he is making arrowheads. Watch him closely but don't bother him. And I want you to practice shooting your bow and arrow. When the contests are held in the fall, I want you to be the best in your age group."

"Yes, mother."

All that sounded like a lot of hard work. But he understood it was necessary. He would make his mother and his father proud of him, despite his bad leg.

Morning Flower found her husband sitting outside their hut repairing the fletching of an arrow. She sat down beside him and put her hand on his arm.

"Thank you for the crutch for our son. He is a changed boy because he can now follow the other children and, most of the time, even keep up with them."

Running Bear was silent while continuing to work on his arrow.

Morning Flower continued. "I know I was wrong when I told you Fighting Wolf would heal and be as strong as our other son. He will always be lame. But I have never met another boy, or man, with the determination of our son. He is athletic within his physical capability, and he is the brightest child in our village. He will be important to our village when he is a man. I know the decision to let him live was hard on you. I just want to thank you again and to tell you how strongly I feel that he'll be important to us someday."

9

Running Bear put down his arrow and looked at her.

"Three moons after our son was born, I knew I had made the wrong decision. He was not going to heal. Members of the Council told me I was wrong. I didn't argue. Other men in the village told me I was wrong. I felt badly I had misused my position. I thought of quitting as chief."

He stopped talking and sat for a while.

"I was hard on our son. I never held him. I blamed you for my decision. A few moons ago, I began to realize that our son was special in spite of his leg. I saw the strength in him that you see. A long time ago, I saw a man in another village with a leg hurt by a bear. He used a limb to lean on, and he could walk pretty well. I thought it might work for Fighting Wolf. I am glad it is helping him."

"It changed his life."

"I will start teaching him other things a warrior teaches his sons. I will not neglect him as I have in the past."

"Thank you, my husband."

CHAPTER 4

Running Bear motioned to Fighting Wolf to move to the right. A flock of turkeys was directly ahead. Running Bear nodded and sent an arrow toward the turkeys. Fighting Wolf fired his arrow a split second later. As the turkeys took flight, he shot a second arrow toward the last bird of the flock and brought it down. Running Bear ran into the clearing.

"Good shooting. We got three birds. What a shot you made on that last one. He was flying almost as fast as your arrow."

Fighting Wolf grabbed his crutch and joined his father. He beamed. Maybe this was the best day of his life. They had been hunting since yesterday and had camped out last night. Today, they brought down three turkeys.

"We'll camp here tonight," his father said. "We'll cook one of the turkeys for our meal and take the other two back to our village tomorrow."

He pointed to a huge tree near the campsite. "Look at that oak tree. It's the biggest tree I've ever seen."

Fighting Wolf moved around the giant trunk of the oak tree. He put his hands on it and looked up.

"It would take ten warriors to reach around it. I can't even see the top. How old do you think it is, Father?"

"The old men in our tribe think it was here even before their grandfathers. It will probably be here long after your grandchildren go to the spirit world."

Later, as they roasted the turkey over an open fire, the scream of a panther pierced the evening air. Not long after the sound from the panther, the roar of a bull alligator thundered from the edge of the lake. A chorus of bullfrogs began to fill the night air. Running Bear spoke over the sounds of the night.

"In all my travels, I've never seen a land as rich as ours. The giant trees have shed their leaves over the years, creating rich black soil deep as twice the width of a man's hand. Everything grows fast and provides food for the deer and other animals. The lake of floating islands seems to dull the cold winds of winter. The big predators like the panthers, wolves, wildcats, alligators and bears feed off of the animals. And we eat the plants and the plentiful game. No place could be better."

"I've heard that the villages by the Big Water where the sun rises claim to have the best land. Do you agree?"

"Their land is good. They get fish from the salt water and dig shells on the shore. They make salt by putting water from the Big Water in large bowls. When the sun takes away the water, valuable salt is left in the bowls. Shells found on the beach are important for trade. They grow crops but get very little from a lot of effort. Their land is not fertile like our land. Think about it. How would you like to eat fish every day of your life?"

Fighting Wolf laughed. "That sounds awful," he added. I don't mind fish from our lake once in a while, but I like our deer, boar, turkey, gator tails and frog legs. I even like our beans and corn. No way would I leave our village."

"I hope you never have to. Now let's get some sleep."

"Father, you said strange white men came to the village on the Big Water. Please tell me the story."

Running Bear put another log on the fire and lit his pipe. "Two years before you were born a runner came as we were preparing to eat our evening meal. He said the white people arrived in big canoes with white hides on top flapping in the wind. They wore clothes and hats made of shiny shells to protect them from arrows. They carried firesticks that killed from a great distance. A small band of warriors attacked them but all were killed with the firesticks."

"What did you do?"

"I met with our Council the morning after the runner arrived. After getting advice, I left with two warriors to a meeting of chiefs near the Big Water. Fish Hawk, the chief of the Manatee Village, listened to all of the chiefs and then decided to send warriors to spy on the white men. Later, the spies told us the white men looked small with weak muscles when they took off their protective shells. They were puny compared with us."

"If they were so small, why didn't we just kill them?"

"We tried. We sent twenty warriors to slip into their camp at night to kill them while they were sleeping. One of their sentries spotted our warriors and sounded an alarm. The white men grabbed their firesticks and killed all of our warriors."

Running Bear paused. "After the battle, some of our chiefs thought the white men might be gods. Two warriors were sent with gifts. The white men took them captive, tortured one to death and took the other warrior with them when they left."

Fighting Wolf listened carefully.

"Did we try to talk with them?"

"We tried but their language was strange. We have never heard anything like it. Then, one morning, they got in their canoes, spread the white skins on their canoes and moved away without any paddles."

"Will they come back, Father?"

"No one knows. It is my belief that the white men are not gods. They are men from a distant land. They may come back. These are dangerous times for the Timucuans."

As they slept by the campfire, Fighting Wolf dreamed of turkeys and strange white men making strange words.

CHAPTER 5

Running Bear summoned Tall Eagle and Fighting Wolf to his hut.

"Tomorrow you will take four warriors to the village on the Big Water where the sun rises. You will take six deer hides, ten raccoon skins and five bowls of koonti bread. You will trade these for at least two large shells for making tools, fifteen dried fish, and a pouch of salt." He looked at Tall Eagle. "You will be responsible for the trade. You will also help your brother with his first trip."

Running Bear turned to Fighting Wolf.

"You have now lived fourteen cycles. It is time you see more than just our land. I know this trip will be difficult for you. Can you make it?"

"Oh yes, Father. I know I can. I will help carry the hides and help my brother with the trades. With my crutch, I can walk as far as anyone."

Early the next morning, the six men left the village for the walk to the creek from the second lake. As they passed near the giant oak tree, Fighting Wolf pointed out to Tall Eagle where he and their father hunted the turkeys several cycles ago.

"We had cover behind those palmetto bushes. Father brought down the first turkey and then I let an arrow go and brought mine down. As they flew away I quickly took another shot. It was a lucky hit."

"From everything I know about you, brother, it was not a lucky shot. You've won every bow and arrow contest in our village."

14

Fighting Wolf felt pride as they continued walking toward the lake. Within a short time, they came upon the swampy edge of the lake. Giant cypress trees towered over the shore. Their roots sent protrusions above the water that seemed to guard the great trees.

Lilies and grasses clogged the shallow water that had turned green by fast growing algae. Insects and frogs were everywhere. A giant alligator slid slowly into the water and disappeared. A water moccasin, as thick as a man's arm, seemed to dare them to approach.

Many dugout canoes were stored at the edge of the lake. They selected three of the best, piled in the furs, and slowly poled through the edge of the lake to the creek. The creek was shallow and slow moving for most of the morning. When they reached the Ocklawaha River, the current turned swift and the water deep; they could use the paddles.

They followed the Ocklawaha to the River that Flows North and crossed to the other side. Fighting Wolf didn't feel he was holding anyone back while they were on the water. His shoulders and arms were strong from using the crutch, and he had spent hours paddling on the lake with the floating islands. He was even stronger than his brother with a paddle. They camped across the river before the long hike to the coast.

As they started the walk the next morning, Tall Eagle whispered to Fighting Wolf, "When you get tired, tell me. I'll tell the other men we will rest."

"Thank you, brother. I am strong and used to my crutch. I can make it."

Three hours later, Fighting Wolf wasn't so sure. His leg hurt. His armpit was sore and becoming raw from the crutch. The pack on his back was getting heavier with every step.

"Brother, do you want to stop?"

Fighting Wolf desperately wanted to say, yes. But instead answered, "No, I'm fine."

A few minutes later, Tall Eagle announced. "We will stop for a rest."

Fighting Wolf knew his brother stopped because of him. He loved his brother at that moment more than he ever had before.

When they arrived at the village by the sea late in the afternoon, they were warmly greeted. Everyone was interested in news from the village on the shore of the lake with the floating islands. The items for trade were laid out for all to see. Agreement was reached; the trading would be done the following day when the sun was at the highest point. The women of the village served a feast of fish and shellfish. Although it was delicious, Fighting Wolf thought of his father's comment about eating fish every day.

The next morning, Fighting Wolf located the fields where crops were grown. He wanted to see if this village grew crops the same way as his village. Maybe he could learn something new to help his village. A woman and a young girl, who looked slightly younger than him, were pulling weeds in the garden. He went over to them and asked about the crops. The woman answered curtly. A few minutes later the young girl came over and explained about the crops in more detail. She said her name was Evening Mist.

"I am Fighting Wolf. My father is the chief of our village."

"Isn't it hard to walk with a stick under your arm? What happened to your leg?"

"I was born this way. I'm used to the crutch. I kept up with five men older than I am when we walked here."

"In our village, a baby born lame is sent back to the spirit world to be born again."

"We do the same in our village, but my mother convinced my father to keep me."

"May I try the crutch?"

"Sure. Put it under your arm, lean on it, and keep your weight off your leg."

Evening Mist tried the crutch and began to get the hang of it in a few minutes.

"Most warriors aren't interested in crops. They leave them for the women. Why are you asking questions?"

"Because of my leg, my mother said I should learn everything about our village, including the crops," Fighting Wolf answered.

"Evening Mist, get back over here and do your weeding. We have work to do."

"Okay, Mother. I'm coming," she whispered to Fighting Wolf. "After the trading tomorrow, I'll show you a new fruit that came from the white men many cycles ago."

"Thanks," he said as he watched her run back to her mother.

CHAPTER 6

Most of the villagers came to watch the trading. Tall Eagle talked with the men about the trade. Fighting Wolf watched and listened carefully. A trade was about to be settled that would meet their father's expectations when Fighting Wolf spoke up. "Brother, don't forget we promised to trade half of our furs to the village at the banks of the river that flows north. They want our skins because of the special process we have."

Tall Eagle eyed him warily as Fighting Wolf got up and picked up one of the deerskins.

"See the special color of the hides. This comes from smoking them with a mixture of coals from different trees that only grow in our hammock. A special mixture is rubbed on the hides during curing to make them more pliable."

He handed the skin to the chief's wife. "Smell the hide and rub your hand across it. Have you ever seen anything so beautiful?"

The chief's wife examined the hides, looked at the chief and nodded approval.

The chief said to Tall Eagle, "I think we can increase our offer if we can have all the skins. Maybe you can make another trip to the village by the river that flows north."

Tall Eagle and Fighting Wolf whispered to each other, and then Tall Eagle spoke to the Chief.

"If the trade is right, we will make another trip to the other village."

After a lengthy negotiation, Tall Eagle and the chief agreed on a trade that doubled the amount previously offered. They went into the chief's hut to smoke and talk about the relationship between the two villages.

Fighting Wolf knew he was taking a risk by speaking up but was delighted when the chief's wife loved the skins. Learning about tanning hides from the women of his village had paid off.

Later, a voice behind him called his name. "Fighting Wolf, come with me and I'll show you the strange fruit of the white man."

It was Evening Mist. He turned and followed her.

Evening Mist chattered as they walked through the woods. She explained how the winds bent the trees in the direction of the setting sun and how the wind kept the trees close to the Big Water from getting tall. They came to a clearing where she pointed to some trees.

Fighting Wolf looked closely at one of the trees.

"It's about twice the height of my brother. The leaves are kind of waxy. The fruit is bigger than my fist and is orange. The fruit is beautiful. What do you call this tree?"

"People here called it the orange fruit tree. They are afraid of it because the white strangers left the seeds."

She picked an orange fruit and handed it to Fighting Wolf. He smelled it, took out his knife made of flint stone and cut it open.

"I don't think it's dangerous. It's just a fruit. The white men wouldn't have brought it unless it was good to eat. They probably ate some then threw the seeds here.

He tasted the orange fruit.

"It's refreshing. It has a good flavor, but it's not very sweet."

He held it out to Evening Mist. "Want to try it?"

"My Mother said not to touch it. You seem okay, so I'll try it."

She took a bite.

"Not bad. But don't tell my Mother."

"The tree doesn't look healthy," Fighting Wolf observed.

"I think the wind blows salt air onto the trees. Sometimes the cold winter nights kill some of its limbs."

"Do you think your chief would mind if I took a few orange fruits home with me? I will try to grow the trees from seeds."

"Go ahead, but don't let anyone see you. I don't want my Mother to know I brought you out here."

On the way back, Evening Mist was quiet.

"You are different from the boys in my village. You have many interests and you are bright. I listened to the way you got the chief's wife to offer more for the skins. You are very skillful."

Fighting Wolf blushed. He had just been thinking that he liked Evening Mist more than any girl he had ever met.

"Thank you. You are also very bright – and very pretty. Could we talk again next time I visit your village?"

"Yes. I hope it's soon."

CHAPTER 7

At the evening meal Tall Eagle was telling stories of the visit to the village by the Big Water. Most of the people of the village were gathered around listening.

"I thought we had a great trade negotiated. We were getting everything Father had asked for. Then Fighting Wolf says, 'Don't forget, brother, we promised half of our trade to the village by the river that flows north.' I wondered what promise he was talking about."

"So Fighting Wolf gets our best skin and tells how it was smoked using coals from different kinds of wood and cured with a magic potion. He insisted the chief's wife feel the skin and smell it. Fighting Wolf had her begging for it. The chief ended up doubling his trade so he could get all the furs."

Running Bear smiled.

"This was one of our best trades. I'm pleased with everyone who went."

Later that evening, Morning Flower sat down next to Fighting Wolf.

"I'm proud of you. You did a fine job with the trade. Did you notice the smile on your father's face?"

"Thanks, Mother. Since you taught me how special our hides are, I thought the chief's wife would appreciate them. And she did."

Fighting Wolf paused and lowered his voice.

"Mother, I met a girl at the village. She was working with her mother in their fields. After the trade, she showed me some fruit trees that grew from seeds the white people left many seasons ago. The fruit was orange colored, and they called them orange fruit. I tasted one. It was refreshing but not sweet. I brought a few orange fruits home. I'll cut one for you to taste. Then I am going to plant the seeds by the lake. They should grow better here in our rich soil than near the Big Water."

"Tell me about the girl you met."

"She was very bright and was interested in the things I could talk to her about. And she was pretty. I want to see her again, Mother."

"Well, maybe you can go back for trading next year."

Morning Flower hesitated and then softly said, "Fighting Wolf, it is time for you to be interested in girls, but because of your leg, it will be difficult for you to find a wife. Most families won't allow their daughters to marry someone who can't run and fight. I don't want you to be disappointed when you return."

"Yes, Mother. I understand. But I still want to see her again. I like her better than any other girl I've ever met."

Running Bear walked up and sat down.

"Good work on the trade, son. You must have a talent." He paused. "Brown Fox has a new wife and wants to build his own hut. He asked for you to help him plan it. I said I would talk to you. What I don't understand is why he wants you. What do you know about building huts?"

"Many years ago, I studied every hut in the village to determine which was the best one. I learned about the spacing of the logs, the size of the hut, the location of the door and the smoke hole. I talked with many people about different roof designs. Since then, several warriors have talked with me about problems with their huts, and I told them how other huts were designed. I guess Brown Fox heard I know something about huts."

"And who asked you to go and study huts?" his father inquired.

Fighting Wolf smiled.

"Mother asked me to do it as part of my training."

Running Bear looked at his wife.

"The things going on around here that I have no idea about."

Morning Flower looked at Fighting Wolf and smiled.

"Tell me a few things you learned when you studied the huts," asked Running Bear.

"Well, all of the vertical uprights should be of cypress wood. Any other wood will rot within five to seven years. Cypress will last at least 20 years."

"To make the hut a perfect circle, select the center of the hut and then stretch a line made of hide half the size of the hut. Then move it all the way around the hut making marks in the dirt. Put the uprights on the line about six inches apart." Use wet clay mixed with dried grass for the caulking betweens the uprights. Use cypress or oak wood to make the supports for the roof. The length of the supports should be the same as the line to make the circle of the hut plus six hands. Use supports for every three uprights and tie them well to the uprights and to each other at the center."

"Palmetto palms should be layered five thick starting at the bottom of the roof. The smoke hole should be about three hands from the top center and should be about two hands across. The door should face the rising sun. I found it interesting that the doors in the huts at the village by the Big Water face toward the setting sun."

"Why the difference?" asked Running Bear.

"For the fire inside the hut to burn without blowing smoke around, the door should be away from the direction that the wind normally blows. In our village, the wind usually blows from the direction of the setting sun. In the village by the Big Water, the wind usually blows from the direction of the rising sun."

Running Bear just looked at his son and shook his head.

CHAPTER 8

Fighting Wolf sliced the orange fruit and removed its seeds. He brought slices of the orange fruit to the evening meal to share with the village. While he, Evening Mist and his mother had eaten the fruit and didn't get sick, he was careful to explain that people in the village by the Big Water wouldn't eat the fruit because it came from the white men. Most people in his village tried the fruit and said it was good.

He divided the seeds into two piles. He would plant them differently because he didn't know the correct way to plant orange fruit seeds. Near the village was a swamp with rich muck on the edge. He dug up piles of it and carried it near the village. After scattering the seeds on the mound of wet muck, he covered them with more muck. To protect the seeds from animals, he covered the mound with an old deerskin that had partially rotted and was no longer of use. He would keep the pile of muck wet and check every few days to see if the seeds were sprouting. If they sprouted, he would then transplant them into the ground where he would grow his orange fruit crop.

He carried the second pile of seeds with him on a long walk to the edge of the lake. When his father had taken him hunting, they had found a clearing near the lake. The land was open, yet the rich black hammock soil looked as if it would grow anything. The winter winds would blow across the lake and not be as cold as the winds near his village. This might be a good place for his orange fruit seeds.

He planted the seeds nearly a finger deep about ten steps apart. He removed grass and weeds around the area where each seed was planted.

Less than a moon cycle had passed when Fighting Wolf told his mother, "The seeds of the orange fruit I planted in the muck from the pond have sprouted. I am going to plant the small trees where I planted the other seeds."

"Where was that?"

"Near the swamp of the second lake. There is a clearing where Father and I saw turkeys when he took me hunting. The soil is rich, and the lake should protect the trees from the winter cold. I'll call it the orange fruit trees at the turkey clearing."

After another painful walk to the turkey clearing, Fighting wolf was disappointed to find only half of the seeds had come up. It had been a good idea to try two different approaches, he thought.

Fighting Wolf cleared weeds and grass and planted his seedlings from the village ten steps apart. He looked proudly at his orange fruit seedlings in the turkey clearing.

CHAPTER 9

After the evening meal, Fighting Wolf spoke to Running Bear.

"I'm leaving early tomorrow, Father. I will be back before the sun sets four or five times."

"I understand you want to explore by yourself, but I wish you would take someone with you. Raiding parties from the Cherokees in the north or the Apalachees in the west come down to this area. They may kill you if they spot you. Even a fully-grown warrior will run for a tree when surprised by a bear or a boar. As good as you are on your crutch, you would be no match for one of them."

"Father, I will be careful. You know it is important that I continue to learn to be independent."

"May the Great Spirit be with you."

Early the next morning Fighting Wolf wrapped dried venison and bread in a light deerskin roll. He added a fishing line and a small bow to make fire, slung the roll over his shoulder and picked up his hunting bow and several arrows.

Fighting Wolf was excited as he left the village and walked toward the creek flowing from the lakes. He passed the great oak tree and recalled when he and his father killed the three turkeys.

As he approached the lake, he checked the turkey clearing and examined the orange fruit trees. They had been in the ground for three cycles and were waist high and healthy. The soil of the hammock is rich and the warm water of the lake seems to be good for the trees, he thought.

From the canoes kept by the edge of the lake, Fighting Wolf chose a small canoe. He added a pole and a paddle and poled the canoe through the swamp to the slow-moving stream. He turned in the direction of the setting sun and paddled through high saw grass knowing he eventually would find open water.

Alligators as big as his canoe lay submerged in the shallow water. Fish jumped and swam so close to his canoe that Fighting Wolf felt as if he could catch them with his bare hands. Fish hawks and eagles flew overhead, looking for a meal in the lake teeming with fish.

After reaching open water, he paddled along the northern shore in the direction of the setting sun. He circled one of the floating islands that changed position depending on the direction of the wind. The island was composed of lilies and lake grasses clumped together. Small shrubs growing in the decaying vegetation held the island together with their roots.

The opening of the creek that flowed between the two lakes was difficult to find. Large trees grew at the riverbank, at times covering the creek with a dark canopy. As he entered the creek he thought this must be the most wonderful place in the world. He found a small clearing on the bank and pulled his canoe on shore. This was a good place to camp.

Rather than fish or hunt, Fighting Wolf decided to eat food he brought from home. He explored the dense woods near his camp and marveled at the many different types of trees and plants. A flock of large parakeets roosted in a tree near him and remained on their roost as he walked under their tree.

He returned to his camp and waded into the fast moving cool water. Refreshed, he hid his canoe under a low-lying limb near the water and carefully covered the tracks made by the canoe. He made a bed of palm leaves and wrapped himself in his deerskin for protection against the mosquitoes. He listened to the sounds of the wilderness and went to sleep.

The next morning, Fighting Wolf finished the food from home, brought his canoe from under the limb and began paddling up the creek. The beauty of the creek was breath taking. Ducks and coots flew out of his path. Egrets and herons waded at the edge of the creek. Turtles slid into the water as he glided past them. Alligators were sunning on the bank. The creek between the lakes was all he had expected.

Paddling against the current was difficult. The sun was directly overhead when he finally reached the first lake. He paddled to the shore and pulled out his fishing line with a hook made from a small bone. On his first toss of the fishing line, a huge bass grabbed the hook baited with a cricket. He tried again and was successful again.

After gathering dry leaves and sticks, Fighting Wolf used his fire bow to rapidly turn a straight stick into a hollowed out piece of wood. Within seconds a wisp of smoke turned into a spark and then a flame. While he roasted the two fish over the flames, he chopped down a palmetto tree and cut out the heart for his meal. He collected a few walnuts and found some blueberries. As he was enjoying his feast, he thought about Evening Mist. She would enjoy this land.

The trip around the first lake took two days of slow paddling and occasional stops for hunting and exploring. The return on the creek between the lakes was easy as the canoe was floating with the current. Fighting Wolf turned the canoe to the right when he entered the second lake and headed toward the setting sun. The floating islands had shifted position; it would be easy to get lost as the islands shifted in the wind.

At the far western end of the lake, he beached and hid the canoe and struck out on foot. The great prairie that he had heard about for years was a one-day walk. He knew the walk would be difficult, but the pain would be worth it if he could find the prairie. He pushed himself hard and reached the prairie as the sun set. He was breathless as he looked out at the vast expanse of land without trees. It looked as if it went on forever.

Part of the prairie was spongy but large areas were dry and hard. Great flocks of birds were in the air. Deer were grazing nearby. Hundreds of buffalo were grazing in the distance. Even from the edge of the prairie he knew it was everything and more than he expected. He set up camp and dreamed about exploring the prairie the next day.

Before sunrise, Fighting Wolf walked farther into the prairie. It was teeming with wildlife. He thought again of Evening Mist. She would be amazed at this place. He decided to walk into the prairie for a few hours and then start back. A bobcat scurried from some low bushes. Deer trotted away and started grazing again. A flock of sandhill cranes squawked loudly and flew off.

Then his heart froze. He dropped to the ground. In the distance, three men were moving around an overnight camp. They were not Timucuans. They could be Cherokees from the north, Apalachees from the west or other Indians from the south. If he were spotted, they might kill him.

CHAPTER 10

They hadn't seen him. If he were not crippled, he could easily outrun them to his canoe. But he didn't have that choice. They would catch him quickly. The only solution would be to slip away. He began crawling back out of the prairie.

Crawling was slow and painful. Every few minutes, he would look up. The men were still in camp. He felt there was a chance he could make it to the end of the prairie and into the pine forest without being seen. However, because he was dragging his crutch, he could not hide his tracks. If they came this way, they would see his tracks and follow him.

After three hours of crawling Fighting Wolf was definitely closer to the pine forest. Another couple of hours would get him there. He looked up. The men were walking toward him. They didn't seem to be in a hurry, so they hadn't spotted him or his tracks.

He crawled as fast as he could in spite of the pain. He looked up. The men were looking down and then looking in his direction. They had seen his tracks. They were talking. Would they leave or track him?

The men started in his direction. They were tracking him. Fighting Wolf got up quickly and started toward the pine forest, now just a few minutes away. As he entered the forest he looked around. The men had seen him and were running toward him.

He hurried through the forest of giant pine trees. There was little ground cover to hide in. He was still exposed. He remembered there was a thick hammock off to the right so he headed in that direction. There was no way to hide his tracks. The men would be right behind him.

He reached the hammock and entered the dense undergrowth. He could now hear his pursuers crashing through the brush and yelling to each other in a strange language. They were definitely not Timucuans. Fighting Wolf realized his chances of getting out of this were slim. They would find him within minutes. He got out his bow.

"If I go down, it will be fighting, not hiding," he said to himself.

To his advantage, he knew where they were. His only chance would be to strike first, kill at least two of them and then worry about the third one. He waited, bow ready. When they were close he quickly raised up. Two of the warriors had their bows ready and the third had an ax raised for action. He quickly sent an arrow into the first warrior, notched a second arrow and struck the second warrior in the chest.

The warrior with the ax threw it at him as he was notching another arrow. The ax hit his good leg and he went down. A flash of pain went through his leg as the warrior leaped forward with a knife raised high. Fighting Wolf fought through the pain and released his third arrow. It hit the warrior in the shoulder and stopped him.

The startled warrior looked down at the protruding arrow and went down on one knee. Fighting Wolf raised his crutch and hit him over the head. The warrior went down on his stomach and Fighting Wolf hit him over the head again.

Fighting Wolf examined his leg. The ax had left a gash in his thigh, but the leg didn't seem to be broken. He bound the wound and then checked the three warriors. One was already dead; another was in the process of dying with blood coming out of his mouth and nose. The one who threw the ax was still unconscious. Should he kill him?

If he left him, the warrior might recover enough to try to avenge the other two. Another option was to tie him up and take him back to the village. Maybe they could learn more about the warrior's tribe. Father would be angry if he brought him back but he decided to do it anyway. Maybe he could even learn the strange language of the warrior. He tied the wounded Indian's hands behind him, blindfolded him and hobbled his feet with strips of leather so he could walk with only short steps. He removed the arrow from the warrior's shoulder and packed the wound with leaves to stop the bleeding. He also tied a long strip of leather around the warrior's neck to use as a choke leash.

When the warrior regained consciousness, Fighting Wolf motioned to him to get up and start walking. The trip back to the canoe was physically difficult for both the warrior and Fighting Wolf, but the captive didn't try to escape. Somehow they made it.

He put the warrior face down in the canoe and started across the lake. Darkness came, and he continued paddling. He rested and even slept a few minutes. The warrior tried to get up a couple of times, and Fighting Wolf hit him each time with his crutch.

When they reached the tall grass, he stopped and waited for dawn's light. He poled the canoe through the swamp and finally reached his starting point. Fighting Wolf nudged the prisoner out of the canoe and forced him to walk. He was so tired he wasn't sure it was possible to get back to the village. He thought about being the son of Running Bear, the Chief of the village, and he kept hobbling along.

CHAPTER 11

"Fighting Wolf has returned. He has a prisoner," yelled one of the boys in the village.

Running Bear came out of his hut and saw his son.

"Morning Flower, take Fighting Wolf to our hut. He is injured and needs help."

He turned to one of the warriors.

"Tie the prisoner to a pole. Give him food and water and have a woman tend to his wounds. I will find out from Fighting Wolf why he brought a prisoner to the village."

Morning Flower was cleaning the gash in Fighting Wolf's leg when Running Bear entered the hut. She said, "It looks worse than it is. He'll recover, but now he'll limp on both legs for a while."

"What happened?" asked Running Bear.

"Three warriors were camping in the big prairie. I crawled away for many hours without being seen, but they discovered my tracks and came after me. I made it to a hammock, hid and surprised them. I killed two before this warrior got me with his ax. I shot him in the shoulder and knocked him out with my crutch."

"Why didn't you kill him, too? Why did take the risk of bringing him back?"

"I thought we might learn something from him. Maybe I can even learn his language."

"He is a Cherokee from the North. I don't approve of what you did. We'll keep him for a few days and then kill him. Learn what you can."

Running Bear lowered his voice. "Fighting Wolf, I am proud of you. You fought three experienced warriors, killed two and took a captive. You fought as well as any of our warriors could. But I want to tell you this. Your value to this village is not as a warrior. You have other skills that are more valuable. Do you hear me?"

"I hear you, Father. I don't have visions of raiding villages and becoming a great warrior. I will do as you say."

Morning Flower finished cleaning the wound and mouthed, "Thank you, Great Spirit."

CHAPTER 12

During the next two weeks, Fighting Wolf spent several hours a day with the Cherokee warrior. Although his father allowed the prisoner to stay in a spare hut, he was under guard night and day. Fighting Wolf brought him food and water and began to learn his language.

Within a few days, he could understand many Cherokee words. In two weeks, Fighting Wolf could talk with the Cherokee, occasionally having to use hand signs. Fighting Wolf thought it was interesting that the warrior could not learn Timucuan words, even though he tried.

"What were you doing in the great prairie?"

The warrior answered slowly. "We were hunting and scouting."

"The three of you must have been scouting because you couldn't have carried much meat back to Cherokee country? Why were you scouting?"

"We are always looking for good land in case our land has no rain, or our gardens don't grow or game leaves our land."

"Why did you try to kill me?"

"We thought you might have a village nearby. If we let you go, you might have sent a band of warriors to chase us and kill us."

For several more days, Fighting Wolf talked to the captive. He asked questions about their villages, their gardens and the game in their land. He asked about their Great Spirit and their healers.

The next day, Running Bear invited Fighting Wolf to the Council Meeting. "What have you learned from the captive?"

"I have learned his language."

Fighting Wolf summarized what he had learned with the Council. Then he added, "While I know the Cherokees are a great nation, they are nothing compared with us. The Great Spirit has blessed the Timucuans."

"Is there more you need to learn from the captive?"

"I can always learn more, but it is time to do something else. I am through with the captive."

"We can kill him this afternoon. It will be good for the village to watch. In fact, you can kill him, Fighting Wolf. You can torture him if you wish."

"Father, I think it might be best to let him return to his people. He will tell them what a powerful people we are and how a cripple was able to kill two warriors and capture him. A powerful warrior like my brother could probably kill ten Cherokees without a problem. The Cherokee can carry a warning to stay away unless they want to trade."

Running Bear was silent. "What do you think of Fighting Wolf's suggestion?"

Each member of the Council agreed with Fighting Wolf.

Running Bear announced, "I will send him back. We will provide food for five days but will not give him a weapon. I will speak to him using Fighting Wolf to say the Cherokee words."

Fast Rabbit (formerly Jerking Rabbit) said to Fighting Wolf, "When you were born, there was talk of sending you back to the spirit world. We counseled your father to let you live. You have brought honor to our village."

Running Bear didn't remember it that way. He stared at Fast Rabbit but said nothing.

CHAPTER 13

Fighting Wolf sat beside his brother.

"Brother, I've been thinking about our arrows."

Tall Eagle laughed. "When my brother thinks, everyone in the village waits to hear him talk. What great wisdom is it this time?"

Fighting Wolf wasn't sure how to take his brother's words. Were they in jest? He decided not to worry and continued. "I've never been in a situation where the quality of my arrow was critical to my staying alive. What if the arrow was not true and I missed the Cherokees? I wouldn't have had a second chance. What if the penetration wasn't deep enough? The warriors would have kept coming and killed me. This experience causes me to wonder if our arrowheads are the best they can be. What do you think?"

"Our arrowheads have always worked for me. Were the arrowheads of the Cherokees better than ours?"

"They weren't as good. They were thick and heavy without a good edge."

"Well, that should tell you something. We're using the same arrows we've used for years, and as far as I know, no one has any that are better."

"You are probably right. It's just that I wake up and see those warriors coming to kill me. I may never be in that situation again, but you and the other warriors in our village will be. You should have the best. I think I'll try some different arrowheads."

Fighting Wolf collected all the different arrowheads in the village and added several from other tribes including ones he took from the Cherokees. He traced the shape of each one on a deerskin using a charcoal stick. He made a balance scale and determined the relative weight of each one. He put evenly spaced marks on a stick to measure the thickness, length and width of each arrowhead. He tested how easily each arrowhead cut through an oak leaf.

Next, he selected three of the best arrow shafts with perfect fletching, mounted an arrowhead and shot at a target using a light bow, a medium bow and a heavy bow. He changed arrowheads and repeated the shots.

Finally, he sketched a new arrowhead. He knew how much it should weigh. He determined the length, width and thickness. It had to be strong enough to survive a hit on a rib without breaking, yet thin so it would penetrate deeply.

After selecting a good piece of flint rock, Fighting Wolf shaped the arrowhead by flecking off small pieces of stone. Finally, he ground the edges on a stone so they were sharper than any other arrowhead in his collection.

He attached his new arrowhead to a shaft and tried it. The arrow sped true to its target with the medium and light bow. With the heavy bow, the arrow worked equally well. However, when he selected a slightly heavier shaft, the arrowhead cracked when it hit the target.

He realized the arrowhead would work well with any size bow but not with a heavy bow and a heavy shaft. After a redesign of the arrowhead and more trials, he now had two arrowheads: one for a light or medium shaft and one for a heavy shaft.

Fighting Wolf brought two arrows with the new arrowheads to his brother. "Brother, try these new arrowheads for me. I think you'll like them."

"What do our flint knappers say about them?"

Fighting Wolf laughed. "They say I should stick with the arrowheads we've always used."

Tall Eagle reached over and took the arrowheads Fighting Wolf offered. "I'll try them on our next hunt."

———————

The hunting party returned with a huge buck tied to a pole. They dropped the buck in front of the village on-lookers and received many compliments. Tall Eagle came over to Fighting Wolf.

"You're going to like this. My two buddies ridiculed me for the new arrowheads. When we saw the buck, I took a shot from over sixty steps. The arrow glanced off a tree behind the buck, and my friends laughed at the long shot and my miss with your new arrowhead. The buck ran about fifteen steps and collapsed. The arrow went clean through him. It was magnificent."

Fighting Wolf grinned. "You want some more arrowheads?"

"I'll take every one you can make."

Later that evening, one of Tall Eagle's companions came up and whispered, "I'd like some of your new arrowheads."

Fighting Wolf felt great. "I've promised Tall Eagle my next ones. Talk to me after that."

Fighting Wolf's arrowheads were in such demand, he traded meat and vegetables for them. Other villages heard of the arrowheads and requested them. He traded with them also.

Fighting Wolf showed one of his arrowheads to his mother.

"Look mother. I've made the mark of a crutch of my arrowheads. When someone sees this mark, he will know that I made it. I've also made a mark on the base of the arrowhead to show whether it is for a normal shaft or a heavy one."

Morning Flower smiled. The Great Spirit works in strange ways, she thought.

CHAPTER 14

Most families had enjoyed their evening meal and were visiting with others in the village when the runner arrived.

"White men are in our lands again. They came on the Big Water where the sun sets. They are walking north through our lands. They killed all warriors who attacked them. We left our village, and the white men took food but did not destroy our village. I was told to warn all villages. If the white men come, leave your village and hide. We will fight them another time."

Running Bear said to the runner. "We will decide whether to fight or run. We have never run from anyone before, but we did see the white men many years ago. They are dangerous warriors. We must respect their powers."

"One more thing. During one of our attacks, we captured a white man. We are holding him prisoner. But we can't understand him. He speaks strange words. We are thinking about torturing him."

Running Bear looked at Fighting Wolf and said to the runner, "My son learned to speak the Cherokee words in seven suns. He can also learn the white man words. Tell your chief if he sends the white man to our village, my son, Fighting Wolf, will learn to speak to him. Meanwhile, don't torture him. We want him to be in good health when we talk to him."

"I'll tell my chief. Now I have to go. I have other villages to warn."

Before the next moon, three warriors came to the village with their white prisoner. One of the warriors stepped forward.

"We come from the village attacked by the white men. We captured this one, but we cannot learn his words. We have brought him to Fighting Wolf."

Running Bear questioned the warriors about the white man. "What does he eat? Do you keep him tied up? Is he dangerous? How many words have you learned? Are you going to stay and guard him?"

Running Bear didn't learn much. He was told that the white prisoner eats what they eat, he doesn't seem dangerous and they keep him tied up most of the time but also have let him loose a few times. He didn't try to run. They can't understand any of his words. And they will not stay and guard the prisoner. They will return to their village tomorrow.

Running Bear had the white man tied to a pole and called Fighting Wolf to talk. "This is a great honor for our village, and for you, to be chosen to learn to speak to the white man. We must learn about the white men. Spend all your time to learn their words. There is nothing more important."

Running Bear put his hand on Fighting Wolf's shoulder and spoke softly.

"I believe the white men are the greatest threat the Timucuans have ever had. Our lives may depend on you."

Fighting Wolf walked up to the white man. The man was two hands shorter than his father and his brother. He was thin but looked strong. His eyes were clear and bright. He seemed to be wary but not afraid. Maybe he had decided they were not going to kill him.

Fighting Wolf made a key decision. I will learn his language and teach him our language at the same time. If he can learn quickly, we can communicate faster than if I just learn his language.

Fighting Wolf asked his mother for food for the white man. She brought meat and beans, and he took the food to the prisoner. He tied a leather strap around the man's waist and then around the post. He untied his hands then handed him the food. The white man ate hungrily.

Then the white man made a motion as if he was drinking. Fighting Wolf got a bowl of water. He said the Timucuan word for water and pointed at the bowl and then to the white man. The white man said "water" and Fighting Wolf gave him a drink.

After the prisoner had eaten and drunk the water, Fighting Wolf pointed to his chest. "Fighting Wolf. Fighting Wolf."

The prisoner repeated the words. "Fighting Wolf."

Fighting Wolf pointed to the white man. "Your name?"

Without a hesitation, the prisoner said, "Manuel."

Fighting Wolf repeated the name several times. Manuel nodded his head.

Manuel made the motion again for more water. Fighting Wolf said, "Water." Not until Manuel could say the Timucuan word for water and Fighting Wolf could say the Spanish word, did he get more water.

Within days, Manuel knew the Timucuan word for most items in the village and knew several warriors by name. Fighting Wolf quickly learned the Spanish name for each item. Manuel had learned some Timucuan words before he arrived but hadn't let his captors know he was learning their language. He decided he could trust Fighting Wolf and spoke the words he knew. Fighting Wolf learned the Spanish words.

Fighting Wolf untied Manuel and let him walk around the village. At night he slept in an empty hut with a guard at the door. During the day Manuel and Fighting Wolf were together constantly, learning each other's language.

After two moon cycles, Running Bear said to Fighting Wolf, "It is time for you to report to the Council. The Council needs to know what you have learned."

"Father, I know enough of the white man's words to talk to him. I have learned much about the white man, but there is a lot more to learn."

"I knew you could learn their language, my son. Tell us all you know about the white men."

The next morning at the Council Meeting, Fighting Wolf told the Council how he had learned the words of the white man while teaching him Timucuan words. "There is much more to learn from the white man, but what I have learned is not good. What I learned frightens me. The Timucuans are in great danger."

"Tell us. Be specific," Running Wolf said gravely.

"The white men come from a land call Spain, far across the water where the sun rises. In that land there are many people like themselves. There are as many white men as stars in the sky. They build the big canoes and raise the white skins that use the wind to move the canoes. Each canoe can carry many white warriors."

They call their firesticks 'guns'. They use a powder that makes a small fire and a loud noise that sends a small ball through the air. It can go right through a warrior at over a hundred steps. The shiny shell that the white man wears is called armor. Armor is made of a material called metal which will deflect our arrows. The white men are trained to fight. While they are not as big and strong as we are, their armor and guns make them very dangerous enemies."

Fast Rabbit asked, "Why do they come here? What do they want?"

"They look for a yellow metal called gold. Manuel says it is very valuable in his land. They learned about our land from the man call DeLeon whom we fought on the water where the sun rises."

Running Bear said, "We don't have any yellow metal, yet they still come to fight us. Why?"

"They want to see for themselves. They may even want to come and live on our lands."

"Can we kill them?"

"Yes. If we attack with enough warriors, we can kill them. But even if we do, more will come."

"You have done as we asked of you, my son. Our village is proud of you. We will send runners to the other villages to tell them what you learned. I want you to stay with our prisoner. Continue to learn everything you can. Nothing is more important than learning more about the white men."

"Yes, Father."

CHAPTER 15

"Fighting Wolf approached his mother and father. "I am now fifteen cycles old and almost a man. When I went on the trading trip to the village on the Big Water where the sun rises, I met a girl named Evening Mist. I have thought of her many times since then. I want to return to her village and see her again."

His mother asked, "Are you thinking of asking her to be your wife?"

"In another year, I will be a man. If I like her as much as I remember, and if she can respect me, then I would like her to be my wife next year."

"Son, do you remember our conversation when you returned from the trading trip and told me about Evening Mist?"

Running Bear interrupted, "I never heard about Evening Mist."

Morning Flower raised her hand and looked at her husband. "Hush," she whispered.

Fighting Wolf spoke quietly. "You told me her parents would not approve of her being with a cripple."

"Yes, I did say that. And it may still be true. On the other hand, much has changed since you went on the trading trip. You killed two Cherokees and took another one captive. You learned the Cherokee language. You are asked for advice on crops and on huts.

"You have designed a new arrowhead that is better than any we have ever had. You learned the white man's language and learned much about them. You are the best archer in our village and a very respected young man. You now have a lot to offer and should enter their village with your head up and looking proud."

Running Bear broke into the conversation.

"Son, I have never heard of Evening Mist, but if someone like you came to talk to our daughter I would be proud." He paused and then spoke.

"Fighting Wolf, I have decided that you will go to the village by the Big Water where the sun rises to tell their chief what we have learned about the white man. Choose two warriors to go with you. Leave as soon as you can but stay at the village only three sunrises. It is important for you to return to talk more with the white man."

"Yes, Father. I will do as you say." Fighting Wolf lowered his head. "And thank you."

Morning Flower put her arm around her son and led him off. "Now, here is what you should do."

Fighting Wolf and two warriors arrived at the village by the water where the sun rises after two days of travel. The overland portion of the trip was as difficult as he remembered from two cycles before.

This was not a trading trip. He presented a fine deerskin and five arrowheads to the Chief.

"My father sends his greetings. He said to tell you he hopes that all is well with your village and the fishing and hunting have been successful this year."

"Tell your father, the Chief, I thank him for his words. You are welcome to our village. Your gifts are not necessary but are appreciated."

"As you may know, I have learned the white man's language and have talked to our captive for three moons. If you wish, I will visit your Council tomorrow and will tell you what I have learned."

"That would be good. I want you to join us for the white tea ceremony."

Fighting Wolf scanned the people listening to their talk and finally spotted Evening Mist. She was breathtaking. She was the most beautiful girl he had ever seen. He caught her eye, and she approached.

"Hi, Fighting Wolf. You probably don't remember me." Rather than appear shy, she looked him right in the eye.

He remembered his mother's words. If she is homely, speak of her beauty. If she is beautiful, speak of her mind.

"Evening Mist. You shared with me information about your crops and told me about the orange fruit left by the white men. You gave me some orange fruit to take home. You had much knowledge that you were willing to share with me."

Evening Mist smiled. "And what did you do with the orange fruit. Eat the fruit and the seeds?"

"I shared slices of the fruit with my mother and then with my village." He laughed.

"No one died from eating the fruit. I planted all of the seeds. I now have trees that are higher than my waist. They love our rich soil of the hammock."

"How is your leg?"

"About the same. It will never get better."

"Did you come here to see me?"

That question didn't fit with the words his mother had given him. He felt his face getting warm.

"My Father told me to come to tell your Chief and Council what we have learned by talking to the white captive from a village by the water where the sun sets." He smiled at Evening Mist.

"Actually, I asked my Father for permission to come. I am really here to see you and meet your parents. That is, if it's okay with you?"

"Come for the evening meal at our hut," she said as she turned and walked away.

As soon as the sun was low in the sky, he found Evening Mist's hut and approached her father.

"I am Fighting Wolf. I met your daughter two cycles ago during a trading trip. I would like to visit with her again if you permit."

Fighting Wolf unfolded a deerskin. "I have brought our best deerskin for Evening Mist's mother. I brought you five of my best arrowheads."

"Thank you. I am Manta Ray." He looked at the arrowheads. "I have heard of these arrowheads but have never seen one. They are very valuable. I thank you."

As Manta Ray was looking at the arrowheads, his wife, Red Cloud, approached and looked Fighting Wolf up and down.

"I remember you. You came to our fields and distracted Evening Mist from her work."

Fighting Wolf almost panicked. He remembered to keep his head up. "Yes, I was interested in learning more about your crops and your daughter talked to me."

"Why are you here?"

"I have come to see Evening Mist. I was very impressed with her knowledge when I met her."

"After she met you, she talked about you. I told her she could not be with a cripple. With her beauty, she can have the most fierce warrior in our village."

Manta Ray interrupted.

"Fighting Wolf is cripple in the legs but his reputation has come to our village."

He spread the deerskin and showed it to Red Cloud.

"Look at the gift he has brought you."

He put his arm around Fighting Wolf and led him off.

"Now tell me how you killed the Cherokees."

CHAPTER 16

During the evening meal, Manta Ray asked questions that brought out the best of Fighting Wolf. They talked about crops, the orange fruit trees, huts, arrowheads and the trip to explore the lakes. He insisted on hearing about the fight with Cherokee again. He was fascinated that Fighting Wolf could learn the Cherokee language from his captive.

"Tell me about the white captive. How did you learn his words and what have you learned?"

"Learning his words was not difficult for me. I taught him Timucuan words while I learned his words. The prisoner is very intelligent. We learned together."

"Tell me what you learned."

Fighting Wolf hesitated. "I am reporting to your Council in the morning. I should not talk about the white man until I have talked with them."

Manta Ray nodded. "I understand."

Red Cloud interrupted. "Fighting Wolf, tell me about how you prepare your deerskins. The one you gave me is beautiful. This is much better than any deerskins we have."

Fighting Wolf described how they scrapped the deer hide, stretched it out to dry and then smoked it with a combination of hardwood embers.

"It takes much time, but we believe the results are worth it. If you wish, I will teach Evening Mist how to prepare a hide as we do."

Red Cloud nodded.

"Yes, please do that."

Red Cloud and Manta Ray finished the meal and left to talk with others in the village. Fighting Wolf noticed Red Cloud took her deerskin and Manta Ray took one of his arrowheads.

During the evening meal Evening Mist had been quiet. She had been looking very closely at Fighting Wolf as he talked with her parents. After her parents left, she said, "I don't know why I thought of you after you left two cycles ago. You could never become a great warrior, yet I saw something in you that interested me. Now, I know what it is. You have great intelligence, and you will not let your handicap get in your way. You are a special person."

Fighting Wolf lowered his head.

"Thank you. I am just a person who is trying hard to make my parents proud of me. They took a great risk in letting me live. I must pay back them and my village."

Fighting Wolf couldn't believe what he heard next.

"If it is your wish, I will come to your village and be your wife."

"Since I was here two cycles ago, I have done nothing but think of you. When my Father took me hunting for the first time, I wished you could see the beautiful hammock. When I explored the two lakes and the prairie, I wanted you with me.

"When three Cherokees attacked me, I thought I would never see you again. I wanted you with me when I planted the orange fruit seeds. Yes, I want you to be my wife. I want you to be the mother of our children."

Evening Mist picked up a couple of deerskins and took his hand.

"Tonight we will be together outside the village. We must not make a baby but we can be together and be close."

CHAPTER 17

The next morning Fighting Wolf walked Evening Mist back to her hut. Her father was out and he didn't like the look her mother gave him. Evening Mist asked if he wanted something to eat, but he decided it would be best to leave. He told Evening Mist he would be back later to talk with her father about getting married.

Other villagers offered him food so he ate and then waited at the community hut for the Chief. His mind was not on the meeting. He thought about last night: how they talked and dreamed about their future; how they lay together and enjoyed each other's bodies.

He went into the community hut with the Chief and other members of the council and smoked and took part in the white tea ceremony for the first time. Even though his father was Chief of their village, he had never been invited to take part in a white tea ceremony. He took a sip and felt the energy of the caffeine flow through his body.

"Thank you for coming to our village to speak about the white men. We have suffered more than any other village, and we must plan what to do if they come again."

The Chief was quiet for a moment and then spoke. "Tell us what you have learned."

"While I speak the white man's words, there are still meanings I do not understand. The white man has also learned our words, so we speak to each other in both languages. The white man is intelligent. He is strong and healthy but not nearly as strong as we are. If he were a Timucuan, we would not consider him a serious warrior."

"It's their firesticks and shells that makes them such a threat to us. The firesticks are called guns and can send a small ball through our warriors at over a hundred steps. The shells are called armor and can deflect an arrow. Their warriors are taught to fight as a group. They are very dangerous."

"But when DeLeon came here, we killed some of the white warriors. If we had sent enough warriors, we could have killed all of the white invaders."

"Yes, Chief. You are right. We can kill them if we send many warriors to fight them. But even if we kill them, we still have a problem. The white captive said the white men live on the other side of the Big Water where the sun rises. There are as many white men as there are stars in the sky. If we kill a canoe full of white men, others will come to kill us and take our land."

"Why do they come?"

"They are looking for a hard metal called gold. Gold has great value in their villages."

"We don't have gold. Maybe they will leave us alone."

Fighting Wolf hated to respond.

"The white man said they might want to take our land."

Members of the Council asked questions and Fighting Wolf responded to all the questions.

Finally, the Chief said, "The white men have attacked us once. If they come again, we won't wait. We will attack with all our warriors. We will teach them a lesson they will never forget. They will send no more canoes to our land."

Fighting Wolf waited until the discussion stopped.

"I am not yet a man and cannot tell the great Chief and Council of the village where the sun rises what should be done. However, I think the white men are a threat to the survival of the Timucuan people. The threat may be so severe that the Chiefs of all the Timucuan villages need to make a plan together."

"We will talk about this in many Council meetings. We will do what is right. Thank you for coming, Fighting Wolf. You may leave now as we have other business."

Fighting Wolf walked back to the hut of Evening Mist. This time her father was there. "Manta Ray, I will be sixteen years old next cycle, and I would like to return to marry Evening Mist. While I am not the strongest or the fastest, I do have skills that will enable me to take care of your daughter. She will have a good life in our village, and we will have children who we will bring here to visit. Do I have your permission?"

"Evening Mist talked to her mother this morning about your plans. Her mother insists Evening Mist can marry any of the young braves in our village. Some of them will be great warriors. But as we talked more, we agreed a marriage between our villages would be good. It would bring the villages closer together. We know of your many skills and understand she would have a good life. I will talk to our Chief this afternoon because the marriage is outside the village. I think he will agree."

Later in the day, Fighting Wolf was talking to others about his fight with the Cherokees when Evening Mist interrupted and threw herself into his arms. "Father says we can marry next year."

CHAPTER 18

While the walking part of the trip back to his village was painful, Fighting Wolf's spirits were so high he didn't notice the pain. He and Evening Mist were going to have a life together. He felt like singing – and he did.

When he returned to his village, he met with his mother and father in their hut.

"Father, the chief of the village by the Big Water where the sun rises thanks you for the gifts. He said to tell you we are welcome in his village at any time. I extended an invitation in your name to visit our village."

Running Bear nodded.

"Of course, he and his people are welcome here. Did you talk to their Council about the white man?"

"I did. They said if the white man comes again, they would attack with all their warriors. I suggested the decision to attack should be made by all the chiefs. I don't think he considered my suggestion."

"I hope the Chiefs can meet before he can create even more of a problem for us."

Morning Flower interrupted.

"Enough of the talk about white men and war. Did you see Evening Mist?"

Fighting Wolf tried to look serious but couldn't keep a grin off his face.

"Mother, she is more beautiful than I remembered. And just as smart. I asked her to be my wife."

Morning Flower leaned forward. "And?"

"We are to be married in one cycle from now."

Morning Flower got up and embraced her son. Running Bear wrapped them both in a bear hug.

Morning Flower asked, "Did her parent like their gifts?"

Fighting Wolf laughed.

"I was really worried about her mother. She didn't want Evening Mist to see me. Then she looked at the deerskin and things began to change. When both parents left us in the hut and took their gifts with them, I knew they were okay. Your advice did it, Mother."

She gave him another hug. "Now we have a wedding to plan."

Running Bear grinned and said, "You must pick a spot for your hut. Your brother and I will help you build it. I know you don't need advice how to build it."

"I've already got a spot picked out. And I would like your help."

"Your job with the white man is not over. You must continue to be with him until you have learned everything he knows. He now knows many of our words, but we can't talk to him very well. It is up to you."

CHAPTER 19

Fighting Wolf walked over to Manuel's hut and yelled, "Manuel, I'm back. Wake up. We've got work to do."

Manuel came out of the hut still rubbing sleep from his eyes. "Welcome back, Fighting Wolf. I've missed talking with you. How was your trip?"

"The trip was worth the difficult walk. I'm going to be married next cycle to the most beautiful girl in the world."

"Congratulations." He shook Fighting Wolf's hand.

Fighting Wolf didn't understand the handshake so he gave Manuel an embrace.

"Tell me more about this beautiful girl."

"She is the most beautiful girl I have ever seen, but it is not her beauty that makes her different. She is very bright and speaks directly about what she is thinking. She is a special girl."

"When can I meet her?"

"Not for another cycle. I will go to her village to marry her. Then we will return here to live. You would not be welcome in the village that DeLeon attacked. You will see her when we return here."

"I look forward to it."

"Today, we are going to get you a bow and arrow and teach you to shoot. It's time you learn to hunt to provide for yourself and help the village."

Fighting Wolf got a spare bow from his hut and explained to Manuel how a bow is made. "First, you select the right size knot-free limb from a hickory tree. The wood must be placed in a hut for over a year to dry. Then you shape the bow with a flint knife. This takes a long time - usually more than ten suns. It is thicker in the middle and gets thinner toward the ends. You take off enough wood so that you can pull the bow back and hold it steady and still have enough power for the arrow to kill a bear at thirty steps. The shaft of the arrow can be made from several different kinds of wood. It must be straight. Any bend in the arrow will cause it to go off target. Our men shape arrows with flint knives or bend them over a fire. Use care in picking a straight shaft."

Manuel grinned. "How about the arrowhead? I've heard they are also important."

Fighting Wolf laughed. "Use only an arrowhead with the sign of the crutch carved on it. Any other arrowhead is not as good."

"How can I be so lucky to be taught by the most famous arrowhead maker in the world?"

Fighting Wolf became serious. "We laugh but when a bear twice your size is charging you, it may help to have the best bow and arrow you can get. But for now, you will use my discarded arrowheads. When you go hunting, I will give you my best ones."

They went outside the walls of the village and set up a target of partially decayed chunks of wood. Fighting Wolf showed Manuel the correct way to hold the bow, notch the arrow and pull back and release. Fighting Wolf demonstrated and hit the target in the middle. Manuel tried and missed the entire target. Fighting Wolf laughed.

"Well, I see we have a lot of work to do. But you'll get the hang of it."

They practiced for part of the morning and stopped to eat some beans and bread. Fighting Wolf took Manuel to the crops and explained how each crop was planted and cared for. He showed Manuel the hut where the crops were stored after they were harvested and how they are distributed to all people in the village.

He took him on long walks through the hammocks and showed him how to harvest the center of the cabbage palm. They looked at tracks of deer, wolf, bear, pigs, raccoons, opossums and skunks. They even saw panther tracks.

He taught Manuel about the different birds and their sounds and told him about his first hunt with his father when he shot two turkeys from one flock. He showed him the giant oak tree. Manuel walked around it, amazed at its size.

Fighting Wolf showed Manuel the difference between the live oak, the water oak and the scrub oak. They looked at hickory trees, cherry trees, sweet gum, redbud and dogwood. They tasted fruit from mulberry trees and enjoyed wild plums and huckleberries.

"Oh, my God, what made that big hole in the ground?"

They walked to the edge of the hole and Fighting Wolf explained, "We don't know what causes them, but they can appear suddenly. The ground just sinks. We call them sinkholes. The deep ones usually have clear water fit for drinking in the bottom."

As they were walking, Manuel said, "I appreciate all that you are showing me, but I wonder why you are doing this. I am a captive, a prisoner. You could kill me or torture me, but you treat me like a friend. Why?"

Fighting Wolf stopped and turned toward Manuel.

"You are right. I could do those things. Our relationship is complicated. You are a prisoner, and you have valuable information about the land of the white men. It is important for us to learn about the white men in case more of you come to our land."

"My father, the Chief of the village, has asked me to learn as much as I can from you. While I have spent time with you, I have seen that you are intelligent, curious and eager to learn. I also see that you have a good heart. I believe you are good man. I think of you as a friend."

Manuel looked him in the eye. "Thank you. I can say the same thing. You are an outstanding young man. You would be very successful in my land. I am honored that you think of me as a friend. I share that feeling and will do my best to be a good friend."

"I have asked for your guard to be taken away. You are free to come and go from our village as you wish. I just ask you to be careful. When you are out alone, there are many dangers."

Fighting Wolf turned and started walking again. "Now that we are through talking like two old women, I have something to show you."

When they arrived at the clearing where the orange seeds were planted, Manuel exclaimed, "My God, those are orange trees. We call the fruit 'oranges'." We take them on our voyages because eating an orange every few days keeps us from getting sick. These trees are big enough to bloom next year and provide fruit. We call a lot of fruit trees planted in one area like this a 'grove'. You have an orange grove."

"I will call it the Turkey Orange Grove because this is where I shot my first two turkeys."

Fighting Wolf explained how he got the seeds from the village where the sun rises and planted them here. "Do you know DeLeon? He was the leader of the white men who invaded the village."

"No, I never met him, but I know who he is. We came to your land because of what he told us when he returned home. He named this place 'Pascua florida' which means feast of the flowers. Your land is so beautiful I can understand why he used that name."

"When will more white men come?"

"Maybe soon - maybe not for a few years. But they will come."

"What should we do when they come? Should we kill them, hide from them or try to live with them?"

"I've been thinking about that. If you kill them, more will come and be prepared for war. If you hide, they will keep coming until you have nowhere to go. It's probably best to talk with them and agree on an arrangement where we can all live together. Even that is a problem. Some white men will be honest with you, but others will lie and cheat you. You will have to be very careful. I will do my best to help you."

Fighting Wolf put his hand on Manuel's shoulder. "I know my friend will help us."

CHAPTER 20

Fighting Wolf woke before dawn and lay still so he wouldn't wake Evening Mist and the children. He reflected on the amazing changes to his life in the past few years. He smiled at the memories of his family's trek to the village by the Big Water where the sun rises for his marriage to Evening Mist and his family's reaction when they met Evening Mist. He would never forget his mother's words, "Oh my God, she is the most beautiful girl I have ever met."

Evening Mist absolutely charmed the people in his village when they returned. She was quiet at first, learning the ways of the village and getting to know the people. She quickly mastered the special process for curing skins used by the village. She brought new ideas for improving the gardens and caring for the ill. She treated everyone with respect. She quickly learned Spanish and could talk with Manuel in his language.

Their first child arrived one cycle after their marriage. Red Bird was a beautiful baby who after four years showed all the promise of matching her mother's beauty and intelligence. Two cycles later, Thunder Cloud was born. Fighting Wolf loved watching him run and play with the other children of the village. He knew in his heart his son would be a dangerous warrior and maybe even become chief of the village.

At the first sign of dawn, Fighting Wolf silently crept out of his hut to enjoy the early morning. From the hut closest to his, Manuel emerged, yawned and stretched. He saw Fighting Wolf and grinned. "Good morning. Wake up early?"

"Hello my friend. I could not wait to greet another wonderful day. How is my nephew? Has the sickness gone away?"

"Your sister took the advice of Evening Mist and gave him the medicine made from the bark of the willow tree. He is better and slept well last night. Thank Evening Mist for both of us."

They walked together outside the walls of the village to relieve themselves when they were startled to see a brave limping toward them. They rushed to his side and saw he was badly wounded. He mouthed, "The white men have returned." Then he passed out.

Fighting Wolf and Manuel carried him into the village. Fighting Wolf shouted, "Evening Mist, come quickly."

Within seconds she rushed out of the hut with a knife in her hand. She saw the wounded warrior, checked his wounds and gave orders to other women who had come out of their huts to bring her water and skins. She tended to his wounds and turned to Fighting Wolf. "His injuries are serious but he will live."

"When can we talk to him? We need to know who he is and what happened."

"He will wake up when he is ready. We can't rush it. Help me move him into our hut. I'll watch over him."

When they got him on a mat in the hut, he opened his eyes and tried to talk. Fighting Wolf asked Evening Mist to get his father, the Chief. They leaned close to the injured warrior to hear his words.

"The white men came in five big canoes with white skins flapping in the wind. As soon as the white men landed on our shore, our Chief ordered an attack with all of our warriors. It was a fierce battle but bad for us. Most of our braves were killed and the rest captured. The white men went to our village and took our women and children. Any who resisted were killed."

Running Bear took over the questioning of the injured warrior. "How did you escape?"

"I was hurt during the first part of the battle. I remember pulling myself under some bushes and then remember nothing until I woke up after the battle was over. After seeing the white men take the women and children, I knew I had to warn you. It took me three days to come here." He closed his eyes.

Evening Mist wiped his brow and said to Running Bear, "He needs to rest. He can talk more later."

Running Bear nodded and turned to Fighting Wolf. "Get Manuel and meet me in my hut. We need to talk."

A few minutes later in the chief's hut, Running Bear said to Fighting Wolf and Manuel, "This is the day we have dreaded. The white men have returned. I had hoped we could meet with them without fighting and learn more about them. Now they look upon us as the enemy. I will send runners to all villages and request a meeting of the chiefs. But it will be up to us to recommend to the chiefs what we should do."

After giving orders to the runners, Running Bear turned to Manuel.

"These are your people. You have been a friend to us for many cycles, and you have helped us learn about the white men. You are free to go to them. We will not hold you."

Manuel looked at the Chief and Fighting Wolf.

"You provided me shelter and food and treated me like a friend. Fighting Wolf is my blood brother. I married your daughter, Chief, and have fathered your grandchildren. This is my home. I choose to stay. My life is here."

Running Bear nodded.

"This is good. Now the three of us need to make a plan. How many warriors do you think the white men have?"

Manual thought for a moment. "If they have five ships, they could have fifty to one hundred soldiers on each ship. They might have as many as five hundred soldiers or as few as two hundred fifty."

"If all villages agree, we can have over one thousand warriors together in 10 suns. Can we defeat them?" The chief looked at Manuel.

"In hand-to-hand fighting, one warrior could defeat two or maybe three Spanish soldiers. But because of their guns, armor and training on how to fight as a unit, they are very dangerous. The only way we could defeat them would be to surprise them. Since they have already been attacked, they will be on guard. It will not be easy to surprise them. Even if we did kill them all, next time they will send ten ships. "

Running Bear nodded. "I have heard you say that before. What do you suggest we do?"

"I can think of only two choices. We can negotiate and agree to help them if they let us live as we always have. Or, we can send small groups of warriors to harass them. Maybe they will move to a location safer to them. Either choice doesn't solve our problem. It only buys time."

After much discussion, they agreed to recommend to the chiefs that they negotiate. They would offer help to the white men by providing food and advice about living in this land. In return, they would ask the white men to stay away from their villages.

"It is my duty to go meet with the white men," Manuel volunteered.

Fighting Wolf looked concerned. "What will the Spanish think when they learn you live with us, are married to one of us and want to return here? Will they think you joined the enemy? Will they force you to stay with them?"

"I cannot answer your question, Fighting Wolf. It is possible I will be forced to stay with them."

"I am the person who should meet with the Spanish. I am the son of the Chief and am on the Council. I speak Spanish and can easily talk with them. I am cripple and obviously not a threat."

Running Bear rose. "I will think more about this."

CHAPTER 21

Over forty chiefs met in a clearing near the village. Evening Mist helped Morning Flower make the drink for the White Tea Ceremony. After the White Tea Ceremony, Running Bear introduced the warrior who survived the battle at the Big Water where the sun rises.

The warrior told his story and answered the many questions asked by the chiefs. The mood was solemn. All the chiefs agreed on the severity of the threat. After much discussion, the chiefs were evenly divided on whether to conduct a total war against the white men or to negotiate.

Running Bear introduced Manuel to the chiefs. He explained to the chiefs how Manuel was captured and brought to the village. He shared how Fighting Wolf learned the white man's language and how they became friends and then blood brothers.

"I even gave my daughter in marriage to Manuel. I trust Manuel just as I do my two sons."

Manuel told the chiefs about the white men, how they fight, their weapons, and their organization. He also explained there were honest white men who could be trusted and others who would lie and steal. The white men would force the Timucuans to accept their God. Manuel answered the many questions asked by the chiefs.

On the second day of the Council, Running Bear spoke.

"We have discussed war and negotiations. I have listened to your words and they are wise. Before you came, I had a chance to think more about our problem. I recommend we send Fighting Wolf to negotiate with the white men. Fighting Wolf would be authorized to offer our help and support to the white men."

"We could supply them with food for a cycle while we show them how to live in this land. In return, we would require them to stay away from our villages and our hunting grounds. I make this recommendation with a sad heart. When we sent three braves to negotiate with DeLeon, they were captured and tortured. The same could happen to my son. However, if there is a chance to talk with the white men, Fighting Wolf is the man to do it. He speaks their language, is the son of a chief, is physically non-threatening and most important of all, a man of intelligence who creates respect. The white men may listen to my son."

The discussion of the chiefs continued throughout the day. Finally, Gray Wolf, the oldest chief spoke. "I am proud to be a Timucuan and to hear the wise discussion. My heart tells me to fight, but my head tells me this is the time for caution. My decision is to support Running Bear and send Fighting Wolf to negotiate. I believe we all respect the abilities of Fighting Wolf and will place our future in his hands. We will meet again after the sun rises tomorrow. If you disagree, bring your best words. We will make a decision by the time the sun is at its highest point."

The next day, only a few chiefs disagreed with the decision to negotiate. Later in the morning after more discussion, they agreed to negotiate but demanded that plans be developed for war in case the negotiations failed. A decision was made.

Gray Wolf called Fighting Wolf to the Council and stood before him.

"Fighting Wolf, you have been chosen to negotiate with the white men. You are respected for your intelligence, your skills to speak the white man's language and your honesty. You will represent us well. Running Bear will give you the details of our decision. Plan your negotiations, but you must leave on the second sunrise. Do you understand?"

"Yes, great Chief. I will do my best for the Timucuans."

CHAPTER 22

Fighting Wolf and Evening Mist sat on the thick furs layered on the floor of their hut. Fighting Wolf took her hand and looked in her eyes. "I leave at first sun for the Big Water. I have gotten advice from Manuel, and I'm prepared for the white men. I will do my best."

"Fighting Wolf, listen to what I have to say. I believe in my heart that you will be successful. However, there is a way to improve your chance of success."

Fighting Wolf looked puzzled. "Tell me, Wife, what you are thinking?"

"What would the white men do if you walked into their camp arm-in-arm with your wife?"

Evening Mist held up her hand when Fighting Wolf started to speak.

"What would they think if she showed no fear and carried bundles of the most beautiful fur they had ever seen? What would they think if she looked them in the eye and spoke Spanish to them? I believe they would be so surprised, they would listen carefully to what we had to say."

"The white men would be dazzled by your intelligence and beauty, but I will not risk your life. You must stay here and take care of our children."

"You are right, my husband. I must first think of our children." She paused. "I must also think of the all of the children in the village. I must also think of all of the children in all other Timucuan villages."

Fighting Wolf was silent.

"You are correct that we represent all of the Timucuans, not just ourselves. The white men would be amazed to see us walk in together.

But my heart will not allow you to be put at risk. The white men have already killed, tortured and captured our brothers and sisters. They may do the same to me, but I can not let them have you."

She stood up and put her hands on his shoulders. "Thank you for those feelings. I am blessed you are my husband. When I was a girl, never did I think I would have a husband such as you. But now is the time for you to do what is right for the Timucuans, not just for me. I know you will make the right decision."

She left the hut to give him time to think.

"They are back," shouted Red Bird. "Mommy and Daddy are back." She ran out to them as the small group entered the walls of the village. Within seconds the entire village gathered around the group.

Fighting Wolf raised his hand and turned to his father.

"Chief, we spent five suns talking with the white men. We agreed to help them live in this land, and their chief said they would leave us alone in peace. They have released the prisoners they took from the village by the Big Water."

Running Bear smiled. "Welcome home my son and daughter. Fighting Wolf, as soon as Morning Flower can prepare the white tea, the Council will meet to hear your story."

He looked at Evening Mist. "You will join us; we need to hear your stories, too. I also want Manuel to come."

Evening Mist declined to take part in the White Tea Ceremony even though it was offered. She sat quietly by her husband. After drinking the white tea, Running Bear nodded to Fighting Wolf.

"It took over two suns to reach the Big Water. As usual, I was slow and held us back. The two warriors who went with us carried the heavy furs within a short distance of the white man's camp. They stayed hidden as Evening Mist and I carried the furs to the white men. A scout saw us and led us to their leader.

"I was told later that the scout had orders to shoot any Indian on sight. When he saw a cripple and a beautiful woman, he decided not to shoot but to take us into the camp."

Fighting Wolf turned to Evening Mist, "You were right to convince me to take you. Without you, I would have been shot without an opportunity to speak."

Fighting Wolf continued. "The leader asked the scout if he saw other Indians. I interrupted and told them two warriors came with us but they are staying away. You should have seen their expressions when I spoke in Spanish. The leader asked how I learned to speak Spanish. I explained how Manuel was captured and I learned his language.

"The leader asked if Manuel was still in our village.

"I told him that Manuel was a good man, and we released him after two cycles. Then he asked if others in our village spoke Spanish. Evening Mist took a step forward with her head high and said, 'I am the only other Timucuan who speaks Spanish.' The white men stood with their mouths open.

"The leader's name is Pedro Menendez de Avires. He accepted the furs but was most interested in the samples of crops Evening Mist brought. They asked many questions about the beans, corn and tobacco. They asked where our village is located, and I laughed and said I'd rather tell them later, after I was sure they were not going to kill me and attack our village.

"de Avires took us to a hut made of cloth and talked to us for a long time. He is an intelligent man who treated us with respect. Because they were attacked when they arrived, they were prepared to kill any Indian they saw."

Fighting Wolf grinned. "They call all of us with brown or red skin who live here Indians. He said they plan to stay and live on the land where they are camped. Many more Spaniards will come.

"I explained that the decision to attack was made by one chief. I described the meeting of all the chiefs and their wish to negotiate with the Spaniards. We offer crops and meat to trade and information about how to live in this land. In return, we want peace with the Spaniards and to be left alone.

"de Avires asked what we would do if he did not want to negotiate."

"Our chiefs are now preparing for war in case we do not return or you tell us you do not want to negotiate," I answered him. "Then he wanted to know how many fighting men our chiefs command.

"I was serious and explained he would not be pleased to know how many warriors the chief led.

"He laughed and said he liked me. Then he turned his attention to Evening Mist and asked her questions while treating her like an equal as he did me. Of course, Evening Mist impressed and charmed him."

Fighting Wolf looked over to Evening Mist and smiled.

Evening Mist looked down and spoke softly.

"The Spaniard said he respected Fighting Wolf and they would negotiate. If the Timucuans could help them live in this land, his men would leave them alone and live in peace with them. He also said he wished his men had half the brains of Fighting Wolf.

"Then Fighting Wolf made a request de Avires did not expect. He asked him to release the prisoners from the village they captured. De Avires explained the prisoners were captured in a fair battle and they planned to use the captives to help them build a camp. He said he would have to think about that request."

Evening Mist smiled and looked at Fighting Wolf.

"Of course, we both knew he would release the captives. At that time, I didn't know if my parents were alive or dead. It was the next day that I saw them and found them in good health."

Fighting Wolf continued, "We spent another four days in their camp. We talked to all their leaders and a few warriors. The leaders showed respect. I heard some of the fighting men say we should be tortured to find out where all the villages are. We were asked many questions about the animals in the land and about how to grow crops. We answered them briefly, but said we would show them in more detail as part of our agreement to help them."

Evening Mist laughed and said, "Tell them about the big deer that the white men ride."

"They call them horses. They walk on all four feet and have hoofs like a deer and are many times bigger than the largest deer. The Spaniards ride on the backs of the horses and can go much faster than we can run. They said they will bring many more horses in the future.

"They showed me their guns and let me shoot one of them. They are easy to shoot and the bullets can kill at a great distance. They are no more accurate than a bow. Evening Mist retrieved my bow and arrows from the two warriors who had stayed hidden. I hit a target ten times while a Spaniard reloaded his gun to shoot a second time.

"Before we left, de Avires made marks on a flat sheet that described our agreement. I made the mark of a crutch on the sheet to indicate I agreed with it."

Fighting Wolf turned to Manuel, "Can you teach us to write the Spanish words?"

Manuel frowned. "I can barely write the letters. No, I can't read or write the words."

"We will all have to learn together," said Evening Mist.

Running Bear raised his hand. "We all have a lot to learn. Our way of life will change whether we want it to or not." He stood up. 'The chiefs are waiting to hear from Fighting Wolf. Let us go to them now."

CHAPTER 23

Tall Eagle looked around the campfire at the sad faces and continued his story.

"The Timucuan Tribe was the greatest nation. More of us than I could count were spread over the country that took a runner three days to cover. All of the other tribes feared us. Game was easy to find and kill. The lakes provided us with fish, frog legs and turtles. The rich hammock land provided crops that kept our storage huts filled to the top. The Great Spirit looked after the Timucuans. Then the white men came across the Big Water."

"Why didn't we kill them all, Grandfather?"

"We tried. We attacked deLeon and his men when he came, but they killed our warriors with their guns. When they came a second time, the village by the Big Water where the sun rises attacked them with all their warriors. Arrows were no match for their guns. They killed all of the warriors and took the women, children and old men prisoners."

Tall Eagle paused. No one moved. All eyes were on him.

"My brother, Fighting Wolf, and his wife, Evening Mist, walked into their camp and spoke the white man's language. They talked for three days.

"Because of my brother, we had years of peace with the white men. We taught them to grow beans, corn and tobacco. We traded game and furs for metal knives, tools and a few guns. We even traded oranges from Fighting Wolf's Turkey Grove. He planted more trees, and his grove produced more fruit than we could carry to the white men.

"If there was a conflict, Fighting Wolf and Menendez, their leader, would talk and develop a solution. It was a prosperous and exciting time for the Timucuans."

Another youngster raised his voice. "The white men are mean. They make us work in their fields. I hate them."

"Everything changed when Evening Mist came running into our village screaming that Fighting Wolf had been attacked by a panther. I went with her and carried him back, but it was too late. Fighting Wolf had lost too much blood. He died. I carried his body to our burial mound near the Big Tree.

"We buried him with many of his special arrowheads, his prized metal knife given to him by Menendez, and even some oranges. It was a sad day, not only for our village, but also for all of the Timucuans. Evening Mist never got over the shock. One cycle later she died of the white man's fever.

"Many of us tried to take Fighting Wolf's place talking with the white men. We couldn't speak Spanish very well and never got the respect Fighting Wolf had. More and more white men came across the Big Water in their boats. They killed some of our warriors. To retaliate, a war party attacked and killed more than twenty white men.

"White soldiers attacked a village near the river that flows north, killed all of the warriors and took prisoners of the women and children. They made them work in the fields. White men in brown robes said that all Timucuans should pray to their God. Those of us who didn't were whipped. It was a bad time, but the worst was yet to come."

One of the old men listening to the story added, "The white man's sickness did more harm than all of the white man's bullets."

Tall Eagle nodded, "Yes. Three of every four Timucuans got sick. Two out of four died. Our burial mounds grew beyond anything we could imagine."

His grandson sobbed. "Why are you telling us this, Grandfather? It makes me sad."

A single tear ran down the cheek of Tall Eagle. "You must understand these stories so you can tell them to your son so he can tell them to his son. We must not lose the stories of the greatness of the Timucuan people."

ACKNOWLEDGEMENTS

Scribblers, a writing group in Mooresville, North Carolina was invaluable in guiding a person, who is more comfortable with numbers than words, to learn the art of writing. They showed great patience in guiding me with their critiques every month for over two years. Speical thanks to Mike, Johnny, Brian, Barbara and Daniel.

"Citra – Home of the Pineapple Orange," by Faye Perry Melton was a valuable resource.

This book would not have been possible without the editing skills of Barbara Bryan. Thanks, Barbara.

Most of all I thank my wife, Aloma, for encouraging me to write in spite of my lack of confidence.

If you enjoyed this story, read the second book of the series – Crosby's Turkey Grove.

Steve Lemasters

Made in United States
Orlando, FL
16 June 2022

18845878R00046